Many thanks are due to Robbie Brennan and Dr. Phillip Smyly of the Maritime Museum of Ireland at Dun Laoire for their time and expertise and for providing access to Patrick Daly's model of the *Asgard II*. Thanks are also due to Simon Stevens and James Nurse at the National Maritime Museum at Greenwich, London, and Noreen Marshall at the Museum of Childhood at Bethnal Green, London.
Special thanks to Finola Goggin (Bosun), Sean McLaughlin and the offices and crew of *Asgard II*. Having sailed on the *Asgard II* in a Force 9 gale, I can say she truly is a shipshape ship! While I have used her as a model for the *Colander*, the resemblance is purely cosmetic.
May the *Asgard II* sail on safely for many decades to come.

There are deliberate omissions and mistakes in the details of the ship in the pictures. These are to accommodate the story. (If I had included all the ropes, for instance, the pictures would be covered in them!) All mistakes, deliberate or otherwise, are my own and certainly not due to lack of help from those mentioned above. Of course, if you find a *real* mistake, I shall claim artistic license. . . .

M-L.F.

For Roisín Law and her tale of a voyage . . . and for Ollie and Oisín, with love.

M-L.F.

A NEAL PORTER BOOK

Copyright © 2002 by Marie-Louise Fitzpatrick

Published by Roaring Brook Press
A division of The Millbrook Press, 2 Old New Milford Road, Brookfield, Connecticut 06804
First published in 2002 in Great Britain by Gullane Children's Books, London

Cataloging-in-Publication Data is on file
at the Library of Congress

ISBN 0-7613-1691-4 (trade edition)
2 4 6 8 10 9 7 5 3 1

ISBN 0-7613-2806-8 (library binding)
2 4 6 8 10 9 7 5 3 1

Printed in Hong Kong
First American edition

You, Me and the Big Blue Sea

Big Blue Sea

Marie-Louise Fitzpatrick

ROARING BROOK PRESS
Brookfield, Connecticut

When you were a baby we went to sea . . .

When you were a baby we went to sea, didn't we?
You, Aunt Alice and me, all three. And a big, big trunk.

But you were only a baby.
You wouldn't remember.

We waved bye-bye, didn't we? Then we were away, just like that, without any fuss.

But you were only a baby. You wouldn't remember.

So off we sailed, didn't we?
There was nothing to see but the sea, the big blue sea.

But you were only a baby.
You wouldn't remember.

T hen we heard a screeching
sound, didn't we?
But it was only a bird.
A pretty bird, up high in the sky.

B ut you were only a baby.
You wouldn't remember.

Then there were lots of
birdies, weren't there?
We fed them bags of bread.
Bags and bags.
You'd never think
they could eat so much.

But you were only a baby.
You wouldn't remember.

So we went for our afternoon nap, didn't we?
Down to our cabins and up in our bunks.
And there was nothing to see but the sea.

But you were only a baby.
You wouldn't remember.

We sat at the captain's table
for dinner, didn't we?
It was very nice.
But when we asked for dessert,
there wasn't any.
Now wasn't that funny?

But you were only a baby.
You wouldn't remember.

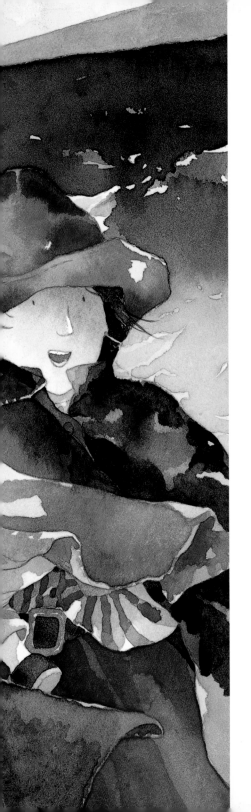

We went on deck for a little fresh air, didn't we?
The captain sailed such a shipshape ship.
We knew we'd sleep snug that night,
down in our cabin and up in our bunks.

But you were only a baby. You wouldn't remember.

Next morning we woke, and there we were, weren't we?
Aunt Alice couldn't wait to get onto the pier.
But we were sad to leave that ship—you and me—weren't we?

But you were only a baby.
You wouldn't remember.

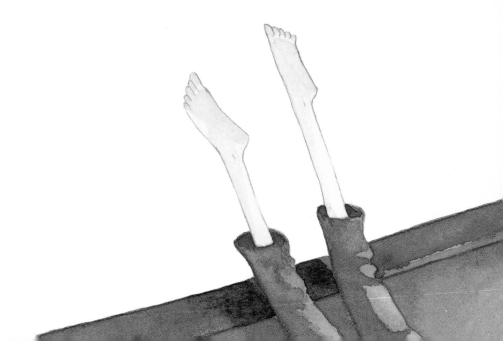

We were sad to leave,
weren't we?
Our feet were all wet,
but that didn't matter.
We were sad to leave
that little ship.
We went home on another
one, now why was that?

I don't remember, do you?

But of course you don't.
You were only a baby.